W9-ATO-933

# CHASING THE GOBLINS AWAY

*for Anne, who knows why*

BY TOBI TOBIAS

# CHASING THE GOBLINS AWAY

## PICTURES BY VICTOR AMBRUS

## FREDERICK WARNE · NEW YORK · LONDON

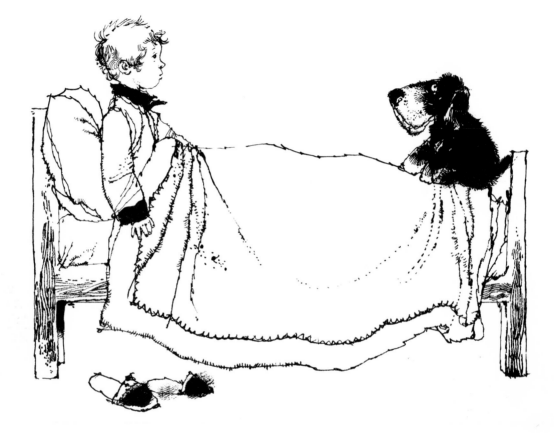

"I don't want to go to sleep, in the dark," I said to my mommy. "Because then the goblins come. To get me."

"Jimmy, there are no goblins here," my mommy said in her sure voice. "There's your bed, with you in it, and your Big Old Brown Dog to keep you company, and your two

chairs and your table with the lamp on it, and your toys
and your books. No goblins."

But she was wrong.

Deep in the night, when my mommy and daddy were
asleep, they came. To get me. And do whatever.

There was the enormous fat, soft, orange one that swallows things, and the sharp one, and the angry one. And then there was the tricky, sly one that slithers like a snake, and the one where you can see his insides. And the fire one, the skinny one, the brown-and-mushy one, the sick one, the one that falls apart if you touch him, and the one

who brings bad dreams. One of them looked just like my baby sister, Nancy. The electric one, and the laughing one, and the lost one. The one made of needles and the one that takes things away. The one that pretends to be your friend and he is the worst one of all. And the one that's nothing but a black, empty space you could fall through, forever and ever.

"Ow! No! Heeelp!"

"Aagh," I yelled, "Ow! No! Help!" And my daddy came running.

He flipped on the light and stood there blinking with his hair all rumpled and his pajamas all twisted and no slippers on, he had to come so fast to save me.

"They let themselves loose," I yelled, "—the goblins."

"Jimmy," he said, "there are no goblins here."

"Yes there are, yes there are," I yelled. "Ten of them. A hundred of them. A zillion."

"I can't see them," he said.

"Neither can I," I yelled, "I'm thinking them."

"Oh," he said, "I understand."

So he pulled the big chair over to my bed and played me two games of Rummy and one of Go Fish. Then he brought me a glass of very cold water and watched while I drank it, until the goblins got tired of waiting and went away.

The next night they came again.

"It's your turn," my daddy said to my mommy, so she staggered out of her bed all sleepy and made her way through the army of goblins and sat on the edge of my bed and held my hand.

"Goblins again?" she asked me.

"Uh-huh," I said.

"A lot?" she asked.

I nodded my head yes.

"Bad ones?"

"Uh-huh."

"What are their names?" my mommy said.

"Snorkel," I said. "Crayfish. Steve. Big Hands. Liar. Swallow. Shock. Filthy. Nail. Mugger. Susan. Knives."

"Those are terrible names," my mommy said.

"Yes," I said. "They're terrible goblins."

"I can see that," my mommy said.

"Some of them don't have names. The worst ones."

"I know," my mommy said.

"I want them to go away and they don't."

My mommy said, "Life's tough. Sometimes there are bad things in it."

"Like goblins?" I said.

"Well, sort of like goblins," she said, "but not exactly."

And we sat in the quiet some more. Big Old Brown Dog watched us. Very slowly, one after the other, the goblins got bored and disappeared. My mommy was holding my hand looser and looser. She was getting awfully sleepy. Her head was drooping and her eyes were almost closed. She's not very good at being waked up in the middle of the night. The last goblin faded out into a grey nothing. My mommy was yawning. She said, in a muzzy voice, "Jimmy, sweetie, I've just got to go to sleep."

"Well, O.K.," I said, and let go of her hand, "but if the goblins come back, I'm going to yell and wake you up."

"O.K.," she said, and kissed me tight.

"Will you come?" I said.

"Did I ever not come?" she said, and tucked the blankets in to keep the goblins away. And left the stair light on because they like the dark. And told my Big Old Brown Dog to guard the door.

And I was so safe I went to sleep.

But the next night the goblins came again. And they had gotten fiercer, and bigger, and more, since the last time.

"Aagh! Ow! No! Help!" I yelled. And my daddy came running. But not so fast this time. He flicked on the light. I could see he'd taken the time to put on his bathrobe and slippers—and he had a different kind of look on his face.

"Listen, Jimmy," he said, "we can't have these goblins running around here every night. And your mommy and I have to get some sleep. So what are we going to do?"

"I don't know," I said.

"Jimmy," my daddy said, "you'll just have to fight those goblins."

"Not me," I said.

"And win," he said.

"I can't. There's more of them than me," I yelled.

"That's all right," my daddy said, like he knew. "You're tougher, and smarter. And older," he said, turning out the light.

"I know you can do it, Jimmy," he said into the dark.

I heard his slippers flapping down the hall.

Then I heard my mommy's sleepy voice, far away, ask him a question. And I heard my daddy's voice say, good and loud, "He can do it. He'll be just fine."

But he was wrong.

I was alone in the dark, with the goblins. I could hear them breathing and snorting and laughing. All around me.

"I'm strong and brave," I whispered. "I'm brave and strong." But they didn't hear me.

I said, "Splat you, goblins." But not so loud.

I said, "Scruff you, goblins," louder.

I said, "Out and gone and down the drain," much louder now.

I yelled, "One two three, gump, you're all dead. Flat and dead and disappeared."

But they weren't. Only the weakest and silliest ones. The ones that didn't count anyway.

The rest of them kept coming. Closer. They put on their worst faces, trying to scare me. Brown Dog began to whimper and howl. Then they all did their horrible things—shining and cracking and breaking and sizzling and staring.

It was like a bad dream, only I wasn't sleeping. It was like a bad dream when you know something awful's going to happen and the worst thing is you don't know what. Only I was wide awake.

They were sneaking much nearer. I could feel them. And I was just standing there, scared, waiting for them to come. And all of a sudden, I got so mad, I yelled, "You're not going to get me, you creeps. If there's any getting around here, I'm going to get you."

And I threw my pillow right into the middle of them, hard, to keep them off. Three of them went down with an "ouff." And so I pulled the blue quilt off my bed and threw that over a whole bunch of them. They were wriggling and fighting underneath, making horrible noises

and lumps. One crawled free and crept away into a dark corner, but a big mess of them never came out again.

There were others coming, though. And I grabbed a skate and threw that, and a softball and threw that, and a whole pile of comic books went flapping over them. I yanked the belt out of my bathrobe and twirled it around like a lariat, and snared four of them, only one slipped loose. And I kicked my slippers into their faces and gr-r-rd my teeth at the one with the slimy smile.

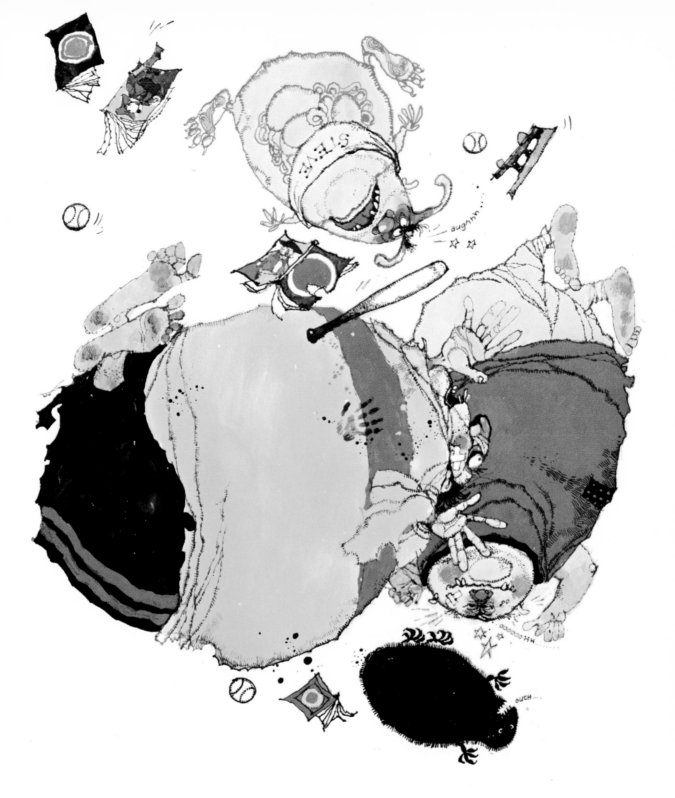

Half of them were down now, but the other half were waiting. And laughing without any sound.

They were very close and very big. And they were making a circle around me. I stood up on my bed taller than the tallest one. But then that tall one stretched and reached and grew, all green and shimmering, until his ugly head was up to the ceiling. He was bigger than me. Bigger than my daddy and mommy. Bigger than anyone.

"Help, Brown Dog, help," I screamed. Brown Dog barked and snarled and snapped at the Tall One's ankles until he shivered and shook and snapped into pieces. He lay there on the floor, like green, shiny pieces of a broken soda bottle, until the shining puddles of him dried up and disappeared.

But then others, the worst ones, the ones without any names kept coming and coming, out of nowhere.

I opened my mouth to yell, but I didn't know the magic words to keep me safe.

*"You can do it, Jimmy," my daddy said.*

"Jimmy," I yelled at them. "Jimmy Powell. You're not going to get me. I'm me, and I'm not going to let you. Jimmy Richard Evan Powell. Jimmy Richard Evan Powell. So there, you dumb goblins, you're not even real."

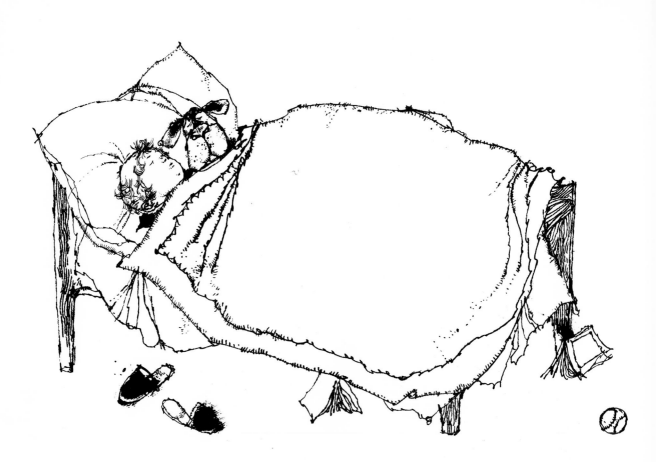

But I closed my eyes tight because I was so afraid. And then I opened them and there was nothing but dark and quiet. And me. And Brown Dog beside me, soft and warm. His heart was thumping and he was panting hard from the big fight. No goblins. I got the blue quilt from the floor and covered us and we lay on my bed and rested together for a while.

Then I said to him, "Come on, boy," and I marched up to my mommy and daddy's door.

"Come on in, we were up anyway," my daddy said.

"I won," I said.

"I knew you could," my daddy said. "We were counting on it."

"Good for you, Jimmy," my mommy said, yawning.

"Jim," I said.

"Wait here, champ," my dad said, and went down to the kitchen and came back with a big pitcher of ice-cold milk and a mountain of chocolate chip cookies. My mommy sat up in bed blinking the sleep out of her eyes, and we all had a celebration.

I got the cookies with the most chocolate chips because I was the one who chased the goblins away. Because I did it all by myself. Big Old Brown Dog got a biscuit I found for him at the bottom of the pile. My baby sister Nancy missed the whole thing, sleeping away in her dumb crib. And if those goblins ever come back, they'll be sorry, because I know just what to do.